OTHERWISE

Linda Oatman High

SADDLEBACK
EDUCATIONAL PUBLISHING

GRAVEL ROAD

Bi-Normal

Edge of Ready

Expecting *(rural)*

Falling Out of Place

FatherSonFather

Finding Apeman *(rural)*

A Heart Like Ringo Starr *(verse)*

I'm Just Me

Otherwise *(verse)*

Rodeo Princess *(rural)*

Screaming Quietly

Self. Destructed.

Skinhead Birdy

Teeny Little Grief Machines *(verse)*

That Selfie Girl *(verse)*

2 Days

Unchained

Varsity 170

SADDLEBACK
EDUCATIONAL PUBLISHING
www.sdlback.com

ISBN-13: 978-1-62250-891-4
ISBN-10: 1-62250-891-2
eBook: 978-1-61247-999-6

Printed in Guangzhou, China
NOR/0715/CA21501088

19 18 17 16 15   3 4 5 6 7

Gravel Road

VERSE

Dedication

For everyone who has ever felt "different." Thanks once again to the Highlights Foundation. Most of this book was written in the farmhouse where the founders of *Highlights for Children* magazine lived. Boyds Mills is my magic place!

Otherwise

We are all
Otherwise.

Bill number S868
passed today
in the state of
Pennsylvania.

Last to pass in the nation.

> And in 30 days
> this will be our law:
> **No Gender Specified.**

No more boy.
No more girl.

Unisex is best,
they say,
for our state and the rest.

The population explosion
has created
a mess.

Control
is their answer.

Everyone must
now shave
their heads.

Everyone must
now wear
the same gray
uniform.

I must confess,
checking the box that says
"Otherwise" or "Unisex"
does not seem best
to me.

I feel like a freak.

I am now
—we are all—

Otherwise.

How It Started

This all started
back in 2022

when preschools
and day cares
and most parents
began to think

there should be no
more pink
or blue
for new humans.

Yellow and purple and orange
and aquamarine green
were cool.

Then nobody had a clue
if that human
was a boy or a girl.

The babies were all the same.

Only those who changed
the diapers
knew the truth.

Nobody Was Given a Name

At the Equal Preschool,
the rules included no tutus.
No doll babies.
And no trucks.

That was totally messed up.

I always knew what I was
anyway.

We had a play kitchen
filled with Lincoln Logs,
with no division
between kitchen sink
and construction site.

There was no difference
between
building a church or flipping a burger.

Making a road or baking a cake.
Hammers or spatulas.

We
were
all
the
same.

That was the beginning
of when nobody
was given a
name.

Not for the
public domain
anyway.

The Future of Neutral

THE FUTURE OF NEUTRAL!

Gen FN!
My generation
has a name.

They gave
it to us, the government
did.

I always wished
to be part of something
better
than Gen FN,
the generation
with a vision of
no gender
division.

I hate
bill S868.

In 30 days,
I will hate
our new law too.

We

are

screwed.

News

The news people
in their gray
unisex uniforms
report the decision.

> In 30 days,
> those not living
> as Otherwise
> must live in prison.

Maybe I'll bail.
Just leave the country.
Flee for Mexico.

> I don't want to go
> to jail.

I shut down
the computer,
not giving a hoot
what the news people
report

as news.

30 days
seems far away

anyway.

If We Are All Otherwise

29 days.

If we are all Otherwise,
are we all sexless?

This is what I am wondering
today.

> Falling in love is something
> that hasn't yet happened
> to me, at 17.

I've stumbled into lust.
I've tripped into kisses,

with at least 6
different lips.

When we are all Otherwise,
sex won't be okay.

My mind is totally
blown.

But at least my brain
is one thing

the
government
doesn't
own.

I Hate My Parents

Day number 28.

I hate
my parents,
who say
that they actually *approve*
of bill S868.

Great.

"No more makeup!" says my mom,
who was once Queen of the Prom.

"No more dresses!"
She shaved off her red hair.

Buzzed my hair too.

And Dad's.

My brother already
sports a crew.

This is messing with my head.

"Everything is okay
with bill S868!"
Dad raves.

"I was so tired of being
a man
anyway."

I don't talk.
I have nothing good to say.

I Hate My Brother

My brother
is using drugs.

Something, but
I don't know what.

All I know
is that he is completely messed up.

Last night
he tackled Dad
in the kitchen.

Got in a big fight
over a stupid frickin'
fishing pole.

And that wasn't the worst.

He cursed
at Mom, using words
never meant
for the person
who gave birth to you.

                              I have no clue
                           what this new
              supposed to be a family
                       is going to do.

I Even Hate My
Best Friend Forever

I even hate

> my best friend forever.

We were born together.
On the same day.

> In the same hospital.

We slept side by side
in the nursery.

I was late morning,

> and they were early afternoon.

The only thing
that came between us

> was lunch.

My BFF recently punched somebody
in front of the Hot Dog Shop.

> And that somebody
> just happened to be a cop.

My friend was never a jerk
before this.

And they work
at the Animal Rescue Center.

But now my friend is pissed
at anything connected
to the law.

And they broke that cop's freakin' jaw.

I am not going to answer
if they ever try to call.

Maybe One Day I'll Be Okay.
Or Not.

I drove alone
      to the ocean.

The same old
      rolling motion
            of the water
                  is better than
                        anything at home.

Seagulls squawk.

I imagine
      they are talking
bird gossip
      about how
everybody here
      at the Jersey Shore
walks around in
      the same lame
bathing suit:

the dark blue
one-piece stretch
made especially
to try
to disguise
gender.

The stupid suit
binds boobs and other parts

(for everybody)
so that nobody knows
if the person underneath
is a guy or a girl.

And every leg must be
shaved smooth.

Bill S868 became
Jersey State law
last year,
so the people here
are
used
to
this.

Nobody seems pissed.

I feel like a loser
in this
new blue
bathing suit,

but being
at the Shore
is worth more
than how I feel.

It might help me to heal.

Being here at the beach
might just teach
me how to be
gender free.

Seeing all these
people
acting okay
on a
so-called
normal day
gives me hope

that I'll actually be able
to cope
with what is going

to happen
at home
in 28 days.

Maybe I'll be okay.

Or not.

Suddenly, summer
feels like a complete bummer.

But then,
        three   dolphins   leap,

                  sleek and silver-gray,

in front of me.

            They're free.

Nobody tells them
what or what not
to be.

And that's when
it hits me.

We can see
a dolphin,
but nobody knows
what it is.

It's not like we
say, "Hey! A boy
dolphin!"

Dolphins all
just seem
to be
gender free.

And there's not one
of them
not beautiful.

Maybe one day
when I'm dead,
I'll get to be
a dolphin
and pretend
to be
gender free
too.

Or not.

This freakin' beach
is
way
too
hot.

At the Shipwreck Campground

I leave the beach
at sunset
and head west,
in the direction
of the Shipwreck
Campground.

I love that place.

It has a pirate face
on the front gate,
and a big fake
shipwreck
that makes
up a
                    mini-golf

                        course.

24

We always came
for our family
vacation,
back in the day
when we went away
together.

I have such great
memories
from that place.

When I see
the pirate face,
it actually makes
me cry
a couple of tears,
thinking of all
those years.

So here I am,
driving through the
pirate-face gate
of the Shipwreck Campground.

I love to sleep
under stars.
So I always keep
a sleeping bag
in my car,
just in case.

I also always
keep a tent
on the seat
of my 1963
neon-green,
über-antique
Volkswagen Beetle.

"Cool car," says a unisex human at the gate.

"Thanks," I say.

I pay
for one night
at a campsite.

Everything
is going to be
all right
now that I am here.

Maybe somebody
will have beer
like last year,
when I came here
alone.

I pick up my phone
and text home,

"At the Shipwreck Campground."

At the Campsite

At the campsite,
      I fight
      the urge
            to just pack up
            and go home.

I'm so lonely, and it's only me

            beneath the sky.

              The moon
              is a circle,
                full.

Stars sparkle
      and fall,
            but there's
              a wall
              between me
              and being
              happy.

I'm feeling crappy.
The fire crackles and
snaps,

wood burning
to ash
before my eyes.

I'm tired.
If I had enough money,
I'd just run
to the campground store
and buy enough stuff
to make s'mores.

I'm broke now, though.

I'm more broke—
breaking, broken—
than anybody
knows.

Boy or Girl?

The campfire dies,
crackles,
down to sparks
and embers,
and I remember
fires
from days gone by.

This is campsite number 5.

We—our family—
stayed here before.

I know the trees
and their leaves
by heart.

I know this
big rock,
and that rut,

and the way
those old roots

tangle and bend
behind the tent.

I know
the sounds
of the campground.

Stacking of wood.
Snapping of fire.
Trickle of creek.

Happy families
shrieking
with kids.

I know
the rustle
of leaves
in wind,

and the
crack of twigs
beneath feet.

It is all
the same
on this day 28.

But then

there is something new.

Whistling,
so good
that it could
be half-person,
half-bird.

It seems to be
from the site
next
to me.

"Hello?" I call,
all fake-happy
and brave.

"Hey," a voice says.

A shadow
moves through
the night,

and in the light
of the fire

I see the face.

It seems to be
a teen like me.

The head is shaved,
a fuzzy buzz,

and the eyes are
full of light,
even in the dark
of night.

They seem to
be green.

And they
glisten that light
right toward
me.

"Well, hello,"
says this person.

My mind is
bursting
with the question:

girl or boy?

You can no longer
tell by
the voice
because the government
requires all citizens

to ingest the medicine
to make voices
sound the same.

The unisex uniform
hides the bodies,
of course.

There's nothing
worse—

in my opinion—

than having
that
constant question
in your head:

boy or girl?

It whirls and
swirls
until
your entire mind
and eyes
are occupied

with trying

to find
the right
answer.

Name

"What's your name?"

I ask the face,
breaking the law.

Nobody is supposed
to know anybody's
name

because that might
make
them take
a guess
at gender.

"Whistler,"
the lips whisper.

"And you?"

I don't know what to do.
I have a pre-Equal Preschool
name from birth.

But my name gives away
what I am.

It is gender-specific,
and I know
I could go
to prison

for revealing it
to anybody
not known
from long ago.

This person
could even be
a worker
from the government.

I stare
at the dying fire.

I make up a lie
of a brand-new name.

"Spark," I say.
"My name is Spark."

Whistler reaches
out a hand.

I do the same.

We shake.

The touch of flesh

    against flesh

        gives me a shiver,

           and something

               deep within me

                q
                  u
                    i
                      v
                        e
                          r
                            s.

Whistler and Spark

So here we are,
Whistler and Spark,

just two humans
below zillions of stars.

Whistler sits on
the big rock.

I find
a nice spot
to put out my sleeping
bag.

I haven't even
set up the tent
yet.

"Your accent,"
Whistler says.

"You're not
from around
here."

"Pennsylvania,"
I say.
"Just three hours
away.

Where do
you live?"
I ask,

and Whistler
laughs.

"I live
wherever I
am."

"So you have no home?"

"My home
is wherever
I go."

"Oh-kay," I say.

I've heard
of Jersey drifters,
gypsies,

people who
move from

                             one place

to another

                             across the state.

It all started,
they say,
with the passing
of bill S868,

when
lots of parents
killed themselves
and left
     little kids
          behind.

I almost ask
if Whistler
is one of those
suicide victims' kids.

But then
the editor
in my head
kicks in.

So instead
I ask another
question in
my head.

                "How old are you?"

"Seventeen,"
Whistler says.

"And you?"

                    "Me too."

I rub my smooth
head
and shiver
inside this stupid
unisex uniform,

feeling
suddenly awkward
and shy.

            I feel as if
                I am swimming
                        inside
                            of Whistler's eyes,

making waves
and shaking up
everything
inside of me.

Yum

Whistler has brought
marshmallows, chocolate,
graham crackers, hot dogs,
fruit snacks … and whiskey.

I listen as Whistler whistles
through the trees
to retrieve
all this stuff.

If Whistler is a gypsy or a drifter,
where does the money come from?

The idea hits me
that maybe Whistler is a thief.
But a person
has to survive,
so I can deal with stealing.

But
what if Whistler is a killer?

I could be dead.

I shake that thought out of
my head.

There are no murderer
vibes
in those eyes.

Whistler's eyes
are kind.

I
really
like
those
eyes.

And that face,
and the way
Whistler moves.

I'm grooving
on all these
reflections
of what
I like best

about this person
when Whistler
returns.

     "Bon appétit!
         Let's eat!"

Whistler rekindles
the fire,
and we roast
hot dogs
on sticks,

taking shots
of whiskey.

The liquid
burns a path
of fire
down my throat
into my gut.

"What is this?"
I ask.

"Rum."

"Yum."

Whistler grins.

But what Whistler
doesn't know
is this:

        the drink

      isn't the only

          thing

            that is

          delicious.

As If We Are Two Magnets

Crickets chirp,
and the night world
spins dizzily
as we talk,

telling of
our lives
across the fire.

We tell
everything
but our deepest
secrets.

And I keep
looking at
Whistler's lips
moving smooth
through stories.

When Whistler smiles,
the eyes crinkle at the
corners,

and dimples crease
into no-pimpled cheeks.

Whistler's laugh
is great and
contagious.

It makes me
laugh too.

And I'm
trying to imitate
that laugh
with mine.

"Well," Whistler says,

"I'm beat. Time to sleep."

Whistler stands,
stretches,
takes some steps,
        and the next thing I know,
our hands are holding
one another's necks.

I lean toward Whistler,
        and fall
        face first
        into lips,

47

soft and urgent
all at once.

There is the
smell of
rum, and a
catching of breath
matching
breath.

We kiss.

Everything spins.

The insides of me
are pulling toward
the insides of
Whistler,

as if we are two
magnets
that just
can't help ourselves.

Please Be a
Different Sex Than Me

I am empty
and a little bit drunk
as I set up the tent.

Whistler is
gone.

I can't stop
reliving the kiss
again and again
on my lips

and in my body
and brain.

"How lame," I say
out loud
to myself.

"I don't even know
if I just kissed
a boy or a girl."

The world swirls
in circles around
the tent.

I turn my head
in the direction
of campsite number 3,
where Whistler
sleeps.

"Please be
a different sex
than me," I whisper
in the direction
of Whistler.

"Because if you're not,
I don't know what that
kiss
is supposed to mean …

 or even

 what I

 will be."

We Are Connected

I give
Whistler my
cell number
the next
morning
when we say
good-bye
beside Whistler's
white car.

"Here.

Program it

into my phone.

That way I know

that your fingers

touched

the numbers.

Makes it
more personal,
you know?"

A little shiver

      runs through me

           as I take the phone

                and program it.

"Okay," I say
when I finish.
"Now you do mine."

I hand

my phone

to Whistler

and watch

the numbers

entered

into my cell.

Now
we
can
be
connected
forever.

The Way Home

Wheels against road
on the way home,
and all I can think
about is Whistler.

The inside of my

car smells

like campfire,

so I don't

open the window.

I want to save

the

smell.

My lips are

still sticky

with marshmallows.

There is still

the kiss.

I want to save

Whistler

on my lips

and in my heart

for as

long as

possible.

My drive

goes fast

and hazy,

like a dream,

and before I know it,

I

am

home,

rattling

down

the gravel

driveway.

Nobody Is Home

We've lived here
forever,

ever since I was
born.

And it never
changes.

Home is
this big

old farmhouse
with its

wraparound porch—
like a hug—

a summer kitchen,
a winter kitchen,

and all the
peaceful space

that anybody could
ever want.

The living room
is sky blue.

The kitchen is yellow
like the sun.

And the dining room
is white and as still
as the moon.

Wooden floors
have wide boards,

some covered with
rag rugs

made by my grandmothers,
and others

left bare.

My bedroom
is reddish-purple,
with burgundy curtains
and an antique
pinball machine.

My friends
envy
me this house
and my family.
But what my friends
don't know
is that
nobody
is
home now.

No Note

It's so quiet.

There's no
note.

I don't know
where
everybody went.

It's Sunday
morning,
and it feels
so empty.

I turn on
the TV.

The news people

are talking

about a mass exodus

out of Pennsylvania

in protest of

bill S868.

But my parents

don't hate

the new law.

They approve.

And I just know

that Mom and Dad

would never

leave home

by choice.

I go upstairs

and open their

closets,

just making sure
that nothing
is missing.

Everything is fine.

They would take
clothes
if they left.

That's what I
keep reminding
myself.

But then I remember
that *everybody*
(everywhere)
must now wear
the unisex uniforms.

Maybe they
would leave their normal
clothes
in their normal
home

and just go
somewhere
different.

Nighttime

Nighttime arrives,

and still nobody comes

home.

I'm so worried.

I text 10 times.
Nobody replies.

I call again and
again.

Nobody answers
their cell.

Where the hell
did they go?

Why would they
leave me
alone?

My phone
is silent.

The house is
too.

I don't know what to do.

And then
my phone beeps
with a
message.

Whistler!

"WU? In your neck
of the woods.
Missed you
quick.

Visit?"

Quick Visit

I give
Whistler directions.

It takes
forever
before I
hear the sound
of tires in
the driveway.

Opening the
door, I
smile as Whistler
parks fast
and gets out
of the same
white car
I saw
at the Shipwreck Campground.

"Hey!" I say.

"Didn't take long
for me to decide
to take the time
for a drive," Whistler says,
coming up
the porch steps.

"I was going psycho,
missing you as soon
as you left.

How's this for
a quick visit?"

Whistler reaches
for me, and I reach
for Whistler.

We embrace,
feeling the racing
of one another's
hearts,

even through
these stupid
unisex uniforms.

It's Mom
You Have to Worry About

"So I heard
on the news
that people
are leaving
Pennsylvania.

I was afraid
that you'd leave
too. That maybe
you wouldn't
remember to let me know.

And then
I'd never see you
again."

I shake my head.
"That," I say,
"would never
happen. But

it's freaky
that you say that,
because guess what?

My parents
and my brother
seem to have
left the premises."

I gesture at the
empty kitchen
behind me.

"Where'd they go?"

"I don't know."

"So you don't know
when they'll come home?"

"Nope."

Whistler and I are
both thinking the same
thing, I know.

And I fall forward
into that kiss again,
except this one
includes tongue.

I'm lightheaded
with this kiss.

I pull back
first.

"Um, we can't
let this go any
farther. You know,
the whole …"

"What do they know?"
Whistler whispers.
"The government sucks."

But then we're out of luck.
Dad's truck
clatters into the drive,
headlights shining bright.

Whistler takes a step back.

"Just my Dad," I say.
"He's okay with me having
friends here
when nobody's home.

It's Mom
you have
to worry about."

Yoo-hoo

Whistler is meeting
my dad
when Mom pulls in
too.

        "Yoo-hoo!" she yells.

I'm mortified.

My mom can be
such a dork
sometimes.

"Where's your brother?"
Mom asks.

"Don't ask me. I just got home.
Probably out
partying somewhere."

Mom stares
me down.

She doesn't like to admit
that her biggest kid
is an addict.

Mom lives in a river
of denial
when it comes
to my brother.

My mother
can't admit
that her kids
aren't perfect.

"Hello," Mom says to
Whistler.

"Welcome to our
humble abode.
It's not fancy,
but it's a cozy home."

Mom has no
idea of the kiss
that was just
happening.

Otherwise
I don't think
she'd be quite
so welcoming.

"Mom," I say.
"This is Whistler.

We met at the Shipwreck
Campground.

              Oh, and
    please refer to me from now on
            as 'Spark.' "

Sleeping in the Sea

Mom invites
Whistler to stay
overnight.

My brother
is still
not home,
so Whistler
will stay in
his room.

My brother's
room
has sea-foam
green carpet,
walls
painted with
waves of blue,
and a shark
and angelfish
mural.

"This is like

sleeping in the

sea!" Whistler says.

"I dig
the fish."

"Me too.
I love this
room. My room
too."

"I like the entire
house," Whistler says.

"You are one
lucky kid
to live in a place
like this."

We kiss
once again
before bed.

Except this kiss
is not as
intense.

My parents
might walk in.

"Sweet dreams

sleeping in the sea," I say.

And then I

turn off

the light.

I wish my parents

weren't here

because it's clear

that I'd just go

back in that room

and snuggle up

in the bed

with Whistler.

Still Missing

The next morning
my brother is still
missing. Mom's
pacing
the kitchen floor.

"What a dork," I say.
"Leave it to him
to worry everybody
like this."

"But maybe something bad
happened," Mom frets.
"I bet it was an
accident. Or maybe he
was arrested again."

"Or out of his head on ecstasy,"
Dad adds.
"Or some new drug
that we've never even heard of
yet."

My parents have wild
imaginations
when it comes to
my brother.

Except
I must admit
that
it is all
realistic
when it comes to
him.

I *Think* It Is Him

Whistler is still
here at dinner.

And the news people
are still talking
about the mass
exodus
from
Pennsylvania.

"It's him!" Mom shouts,
pointing at the screen.

It is him,
my brother,
walking,
stalking,
with a bunch
of hulking
others.

At least,
I *think* it is
him.

Everybody
looks the same,
like a gang:
shaved,
huge,
wearing the
uniform.

"What does
he think he's doing?"
fumes Dad.

"Where can he go?
No money.
No job.

He'll probably rob
for food!"

"Dude," I say
out loud
to the screen.
"You have no
clue
what you will
do."

We talk like
Whistler isn't
here.

Whistler says
nothing,

      just fiddles
      with a fork.

Getting involved
in our personal
family business
is obviously
not for
Whistler.

      We finish
      dinner because
      people
      still
      need
      to
      eat.

Another Bedtime

Another bedtime
and Whistler
is sleeping over
once again.

"Last night I
dreamed
that those sharks
were
trying to eat me,"
Whistler says,
gesturing to the
painting on
my brother's
blue walls.

"They're so
realistic that
a person
could go
ballistic."

"He painted the sharks.
My brother's a good artist.
It's his main talent.
Otherwise he's a stoner.
Drugs are his
love."

"That's a shame.
What a

waste." Whistler says,
flopping on
the bed.

"Yeah. He's a space
case."

I lie on the bed
next to Whistler
and gaze
at his eyes.

The full moon
strains
through the lace
curtains,
making shapes
across
Whistler's face

as the lace

     blows

        in the night breeze.

"Don't leave,"
Whistler whispers.

We kiss.

I don't even
miss
my brother
one bit.

The Sound of a Shower

It's morning.

There's the
familiar sound
of a shower
in the bathroom
next door.

For a minute
I think it must be
my brother. But
then
I remember
Whistler.

My parents
only shower
at night.

I just lie
there and listen
to the drizzle
of water,

wondering
what kind of
body the
shower is
washing,

I'm thinking
I should just go in.

Pretend that
I don't know
anybody is
in there.

I can even
smell the
soap.

And I hope
that what
is getting clean
is the opposite
body
of mine.

Whistler's Face Makes My Day

Mom is cracking
eggs for breakfast.

Dad is cracking
jokes, obviously
for our visitor
Whistler's
sake.

There's nothing funny
about my missing brother.

But they are laughing
hysterically. My parents
are going crazy,
insane.

25 days to go,
and I don't
know
what's happening
from one minute

to another.

My mother
is wearing
coveralls today,
almost law-breaking.

My father
didn't bother
shaving his face,
so he will be breaking
the law too.

Bill S868 states
that shaving the face
and head
must be kept
up with, except
with those
approved by
the government.

Dad could be arrested
next month
if his face is not shaved.

He *would* be arrested
anywhere other
than here.

But this is today.

And there's no way

I'm not going to appreciate

having breakfast, fresh eggs

and buttery toast,

with the most excellent

friend ever:

Whistler.

This minute

is what matters

now, and—wow—

Whistler's

face

makes

my

day.

Nobody's Answer

I get a text
after breakfast.

"B safe."
It's from
my brother.

"Why would I
not be safe?" I say.

"It's not like there's
danger
with bill S868,
right?"

I bite
my lip,
listening to the
silence of
nobody's
answer.

A While Is Next to Forever

Mom tells
Whistler
that it is
okay

to stay

for a while.

This makes
me smile.

"A while
is almost
next to forever,"
        I whisper
                to Whistler.

I smell
the soap
of the
shower.

And my lips
graze
the skin
of Whistler's
chin.

I try to
figure out if
whiskers
ever bristle
on this chin.

I can't even
begin to
guess,

                        and I must confess ...

I can't even
begin to
care about chin
hair

when the owner
of that chin

is so

freakin'

sinfully

sexy.

17 Days

17 days
until law is made
of bill S868.

I'm thinking
that Whistler
is here to stay.

        I pray that
        anyway.

Sleeping in the sea
of green and blue
in the room
next to me,
Whistler is
my kind
of happiness.

I fall asleep
thinking of that
sweet
face
and the way
that Whistler
smiles.

There's a
teeny
chip in Whistler's
front tooth.

And I absolutely
love
the way
my tongue
fits in
that space
just right,
as if our
faces were made
only
for one
another.

A Tangle of Passion

16 days.
I don't want to
wait
another minute
to strip
Whistler of
those
clothes.

We are
making out
on the
couch:

a tangle
of passion,
smashed
together.

My breath
is fast,
and I don't
know
how long
I will last
in this
position.

Resistance
doesn't
seem
possible.

But then
Mom walks in
and says,

"Your brother is in the hospital."

In the Hospital

It was a gang
fight. And the
other guys
beat the crap
out of him.

My brother
has
>a broken nose,
>bruised lungs,
>two black eyes,
>cracked ribs,
>and slash marks
>across his arms.

"Charming." I say
when we see
him in that
hospital gown
that opens
in the back.

My lack
of compassion
has something
to do with the
interruption
of passion
with
Whistler and me
on the
couch.

I'm such
a grouch,
I know,
but I blow
it off
as my brother
coughs
and coughs.

Dismissing My Sibling

"How's your bro?"
Whistler asks
when I get home.

"Just found out he has pneumonia.

Broken nose.
Two black eyes and
bruised lungs.
All cut up."

"That sucks," Whistler says.

"Messing with drugs
and gangs will
bang
a person up," I say
with a shrug.

"I guess he got
what he deserves."

I have some nerve
dismissing my sibling
like this, but I'm still
pissed
about what I
missed

earlier.

A Little Ladder and a Mattress

8 days
to
go. My brother is
home and taking
back
his room.

Mom bought
bunk beds
yesterday.

She says
that Whistler
can share
my room.

"Spark! You're
sexier than
the sharks,"
says Whistler,
choosing the
top bunk.

I get the bottom.
All that's between
us now
is a little ladder
and a mattress.

Safer Isn't Always
Better Than Danger

It's pitch dark.

"Spark?" says
Whistler.

"Can I come
down
there?"

"I don't care."
My bare
arms and legs
get goose bumps
thinking of Whistler
in my bunk.

"What are you
wearing?"

"Pajamas," I say.

"I got them in the
Bahamas last year."

"Sheer?"

"No."

"Um, will you …
take them off?"

I hear my brother's cough,
and the sound
of somebody—Mom or Dad—
in the shower.

"No. They'll make you go
if they know."

"Oh."

"Maybe you should stay up
there. It's safer.
Okay?"

"Safer isn't always
better than
danger," Whistler says,
stretching
a hand
over the edge
of the bed.

I reach up,
touch the skin,
and just
tingle
alone
in the darkness
of the bottom
bunk.

Dreams

My sleep is
full of dreams
that include
Whistler and me,
like a movie
that might be
rated *R* or *X*.

I've never
had sex,
but just from
my dreams,
I can see
exactly
how it could
be.

Does this
mean
that I am
living
a dream?

I don't know.

I just go
back to sleep
because
my dreams
are the sweetest place
to be.

Best for the
Members of Gen FN

The government
doesn't want
us to love.

Never having sex
is best
for the future of
Gen FN.

That's what
the news says
today, 6 days
before S868
becomes law.

"Soon, any Gen FN
member
discovered
exhibiting
affection that might
lead to sex

will be
imprisoned
without question,"
says the newscaster.

"Teens need
to be
especially cautious
not to fall
into physical conditions
that might
lead
to feelings
of love or lust."

Whistler looks at me.

Those green
eyes lock
with mine.

"We can't be
busted," Whistler says.

"I'll try to hide
what I feel," I reply.

*But what I feel
is real.*

109

I don't know
how to deal.

Whistler reaches
for my hand.

Our fingers
twine together,
flesh meshed
with flesh
as the newscasters
move on
to talk about
the weather.

Shower

Whistler is in
the shower.

I'm stroking
the petals
of
the flower
that Whistler picked
from the yard
for me just now.

"Beauty for beauty.
Morning dew for you,"
Whistler said,
handing me
the wet red rose.

I held it to my nose.

And now,
as Whistler is in the

shower,
I am stroking
that flower
as if it is
skin.

"Wow," I whisper,
thinking of Whistler
in the next room,
nude.

There is only a
wall
and a door
keeping us
apart.

I start to
walk out of
my room.

When
I get to
the bathroom
door, I stop,
hand on the knob.

All it would take
is one turn.

My body burns
with desire,
like fire.

But then I hear
tires
on the driveway.

Mom
is home.

Electrical Currents

"Yoo-hoo!" she calls.

"Look what I found
at the mall!"

Mom has bought
more unisex uniforms
for all.

"Great," I say
as she displays
them on the table.

Whistler comes into
the kitchen,
buzz cut
still wet
from the shower.

"You smell good,"
I say.

Mom shoots
a worried glance
my way.

"What are you two
doing today?" she asks.

I shrug.

"The usual, I suppose.
Eat. Breathe. Sleep.
Watch the news
for what those
morons from the
government are
ordering next."

Mom takes a big
breath.

"You two are not,
uh,
having sex, are you?"
she asks.

I am mortified,
embarrassed beyond
belief.

Whistler laughs.

Mom
giggles with relief.

"Why would you
even think that?"
Whistler asks.

"The way you two
look at one another,"
Mom says.

"It's as if there are

      electrical sexual

          currents running,

trying to pull
you two
under.

I remember
those feelings.
How difficult
it is
to resist.

But please,
do not even
kiss, you two.

Do
not
take
a
risk."

Be Careful, Kids

Mom and Dad
seem to be
watching us
closer now.

I don't know
how
to hide
what is inside
of me.

It is day 3
of our last days
before the new
law.

"I saw
how you two
looked at one another
just now," Dad says.

"There is one thing
you need to know.

Whistler will go

if we believe

there is

a risk.

Be careful, kids."

The Neighbors' Pool

The neighbors—
Jim and Ruth Caper—
have opened
their brand-new,
in-ground,
blue-tiled
swimming pool.

"Come swim," they invite.

"Any time."

"Cool," Whistler replies.

Our eyes lock.
It's hot.

"I'll get ready first," I say.
I go to my room
to change.

The unisex bathing suit
is such a hoot.

What if
Whistler and I
could skinny-dip?

I zip
the suit,
dismissing the
thought.

Whistler is next.

I wait
by the pool,
not wanting to
dive
                without Whistler
by my side.

Butter into Butter

We are alone
at the pool.

My brother
is in his room.

Mom and Dad
are not home.

Jim and Ruth have
gone
to the store.

"Don't be bored!" they called,
waving good-bye,
and leaving
Whistler and me
alone in the water.

Whistler and I swim
together
as the Capers' car
                    disappears down
                                    the road.

I am weightless,

careless,

a mess

of emotions,

like an ocean

rolling out

of control.

I pull Whistler

to me. We

move together

in the water,

foreheads pressed

and lips

grazing lips.

I am drowning

in lust. And I just

want to unzip,

rip off our

unisex suits,

and be nude
together
in the water.

Whistler is slippery,
slick,
skin like butter.

I lick
the skin
of Whistler's
chin.

Then
the neck
and upper
chest

exposed above
the suit.

"You are so damn cute," I whisper

and nuzzle
the shoulder.

The water gets colder
as I grow
hotter and hotter
with Whistler's kisses.

We are practically
melting
into one another,

butter into butter,

when someone
hollers
from
outside the Capers' gate,

"Hey!"

We pull away

from one another

and wait

as the person

at the gate

steps through.

"You two need

to come with me."

It's a cop

in an orange uniform,

with badge and gun.

The

sun has

never felt

so

hot.

At the Police Station

At the police station,
we are creating some
kind of sensation.

> "They were practically having
> relations
> in the Capers' swimming pool!"

says the cop
who busted us.

I shiver,
still in the unisex
bathing suit
that's so cold
in this air-conditioned
room.

Whistler's face
is full of doom.

"What do you two
think you were doing?"
asks another officer.

"What is your mother's
number?" asks another.

"Please, don't arrest us,"
Whistler begs.

"If I need to leave
the state,
I will. If that's what it
takes."

My heart makes
a dive, falling deep
into my knees.

"Please," I say.

"Don't leave."

We Need to Be
Really, Really Careful

They release
us with
a warning,
after calling
both of my
parents,
and questioning
Whistler
for an hour
about how
the parents
are gone.

"Next time
you will be
arrested," they warn.

"That was crazy. Insane,"
Whistler says
as we walk
toward my house,

making extra efforts
to retain enough space
between us.

"I was scared,"
I say. "Please pray
that you can stay.
I could not go one day
without you
here."

Whistler stops walking
and looks at me.

"Me neither. I couldn't
even breathe
without you beside me.

We need
to be really, really
careful."

"I agree."

"Sweet. Because
I need you."

"Me too."

Cross Our Hearts

Mom and Dad
are waiting
on the porch.

"I knew that you two
were carrying
a torch
for one another,"
Mom says.

"You can't keep secrets
from us," Dad lectures.

"My suspicions were correct," he goes on.

"And now if we see
any sign of lust, love,
or anything in between,
Whistler will have to
leave. It would grieve us
to see that.
But the safety of our
child is more important."

"Can you two
promise
to keep this
under control?"
Mom asks.

"Cross our hearts," Whistler says.

I Hope He Runs Away
Again One Day

Mom makes
my brother trade
rooms
with Whistler.

Now my brother
is on the
top bunk.

This sucks.

He coughs and coughs
and sneaks
smokes, blowing
through the open

window

screen.

I hope
he runs away
again
one day
soon.

Our Escape

Whistler has a map
that includes
the United States
and Canada.

"What are you looking
at?" I ask.

Whistler grins.

"Beginning to plan
our escape," Whistler states.

"Really?"

"Yep."

Whistler has a red pen
        and draws a line
                from Pennsylvania
                    to the border
                        of Canada.

"Across the border,
we can have genders,"
Whistler says.

"No more Gen FN."

I clap my hands.
"Yes! We'll see
Montreal and maybe
Niagara Falls!"

"And we'll see
if we can even
maybe
get
married," Whistler says.

And then we can have sex.

                              Maybe.

If Whistler is a different
sex
than
me.

We'll see.

Packing

I pack underwear, clothes,
toothbrush and paste,
soap and shampoo.

I take
my birth certificate from the safe,
along with my
Social Security card.

I write a note to Mom and
Dad.

> Thank you for everything.
> I really love Whistler, and we are
> leaving for Canada. Don't worry.
> We will be fine. Love you guys.

We are
ready to run.

"Canada, here we come!" I whisper
to Whistler.

"Do you have gas in your car?" I ask.

"Of course. It's on full.
No bull. We are really doing this.
Right?" Whistler answers.

"Right."

I sneak a kiss
across Whistler's cheek.
"How much money
do we need?"

"As much as we can
get," Whistler says.
"Do you know
where your mom
keeps her wallet?"

"Yeah."

"Okay. I guess we should take
some. Just so we know
we have enough.
She'll forgive us.
Right?"

"Right."

But really,
I don't know.
I sure do hope
so.

Leaving

I start the white car.

We have our packed
bags, plus my tent
and sleeping bag.

"Good-bye, home," I say.
"See you again soon."
I hope.

I put the car in gear.

"Spark," says Whistler.
"You make me feel so alive."

"And that's what you do
for me too," I reply.

"I love you. I really do."

I look at Whistler.
"Me too. I love you too."
And I do.

Cop

I drive and I drive,
and then Whistler takes
a turn.

I doze.

          "Oh no!" Whistler moans.

I open
my eyes.

Cop lights
spin behind
us, bright
in the night.

After a Load of Questions

He lets us go
after a load
of questions.

I rest
my head
on Whistler's lap,
not giving a crap
what anybody
but us
might think.

The car
moves under the stars,
carrying us far, far
away
from the state
of
Pennsylvania.

Halfway in One Country and Halfway in Another

Buffalo.

Not far to go.

"Canada, here we
come," I shout out
the window.

I yell at the moon.

Soon, we will
cross the border!

I am beside myself
with excitement.

I nibble Whistler's
neck, then check
my pulse.

"You're so sexy
that it accelerates
my heart
rate."

"Great," Whistler jokes.
"Don't croak
from a heart attack.
That would totally
suck."

"Just our luck," I giggle,
trying to wiggle closer
across the console.

Border Control
is ahead,
lights flashing red.

STOP says a sign.

"Fine," I say.
"We'll stop.
Just no more cops,
please."

My knees
tremble.
I can hardly
remember
my own name
or my home state.

This is fate.

Whistler and Spark—

lover plus lover—

parked halfway in one country,

halfway in another.

The Falls

We cross the border.
We sleep
on the side of the road.

"There it is," I whisper
when we wake.
The falls.

Niagara Falls, water shimmering
in the morning light,
a rainbow shining in the spray.

"It looks like love turned to water," I say.

"We're on the brink, I think," Whistler says,
parking the car where we can watch
the falls.

"Ah, I can almost feel the mist
on my face," I say.

Whistler nods
and talks in a hushed voice.
"Listen to that rush of water.

So much power.
So much magic.
A miracle of nature."

"A creation of somebody smarter than us," I agree.

We don't speak
for a while.

"I can't even believe
that we are really here
in Canada!" I whisper.

Then we begin to kiss.

The *Maid of the Mist*
boat floats past,
people in raincoats
waving and whistling
as we sit on the hood of the car
And kiss …
And kiss …
And kiss.

"This is it," whispers Whistler.
"Now or never. Let's undress."

My heart rushes like water
in my ears, and tears fall down my face.

"I'm kind of afraid," I say.
"Of what?" Whistler's face, so familiar, so sweet.

Those green eyes.

"Of nothing," I say. "I'm not scared of anything.

No matter what we see,
we are still the same on the inside. Right?"

"Right," Whistler agrees.

We leap off the hood of the car.

Together we undress.

I unzip Whistler. Whistler unzips me.

And now, finally-finally, there is nothing
we cannot see.

"Sweet," I whisper as we come together.

Whistler and Spark.

Beside the car.

     Under the sky.

          Beside the fall of water ...

               Together, forever,

                    hardly able to remember

               Otherwise.

Linda Oatman High

Linda Oatman High is an author, a playwright, and a journalist who lives in Lancaster County, Pennsylvania. She holds an MFA in writing from Vermont College and presents writing workshops and assemblies for all ages. In England in 2012, Linda was honored with the *Sunday Times* EFG Short Story Award shortlist. Her books have won many awards and honors. Information on her work may be found online at www.lindaoatmanhigh.com.